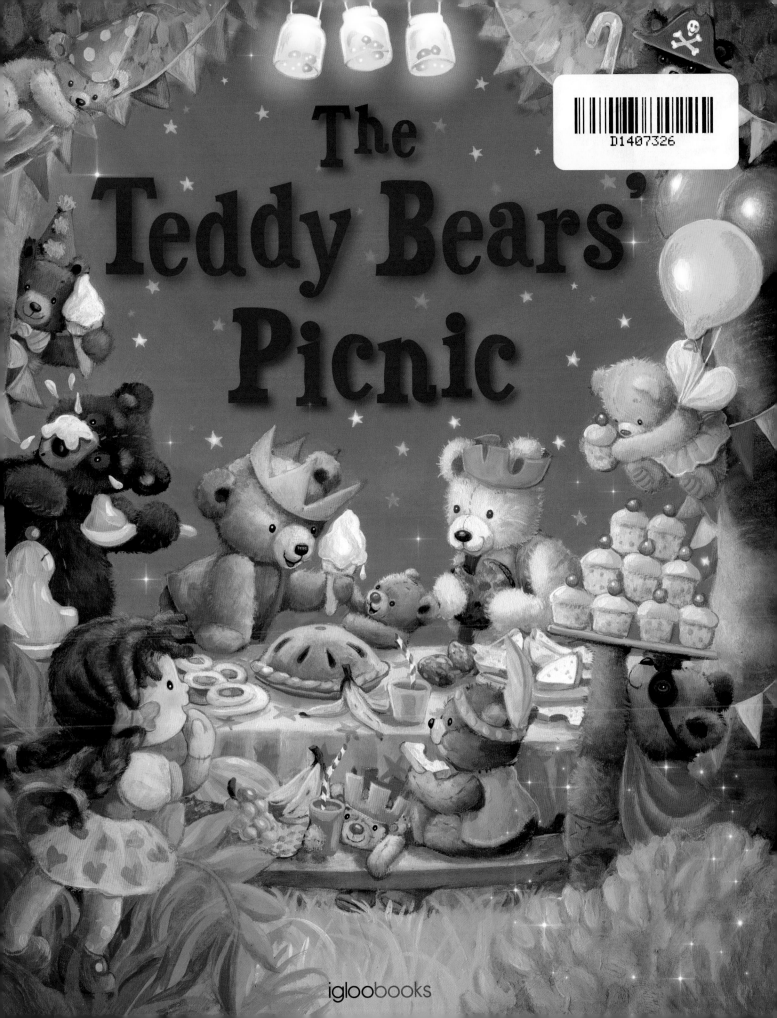

# The Teddy Bears' Picnic

igloobooks

If you should peek through the bedroom door,
There's a wonderful sight to be found.

# This igloo book belongs to:

.........................................

# igloobooks

Published in 2014
by Igloo Books Ltd
Cottage Farm
Sywell
NN6 0BJ
www.igloobooks.com

LEO002 0514
2 4 6 8 10 9 7 5 3 1
ISBN 978-1-78440-085-9

Illustrated by Gill Guile

Printed and manufactured in China

A cute teddy bear is singing a song,
With his little toy friends gathered round.

In the still of the night, Dolly awakes,,
What is the sound that she suddenly hears?

She quietly tiptoes down the stairs,

To spot Teddy, as he disappears.

Dashing downstairs to the cottage door,

Dolly can hardly believe what she sees.

Teddy zooms off down the moonlit path,
Before vanishing into the trees.

Then, all at once, the woods come to life,
There are teddies of every kind.
They join in and sing a beautiful song,
As Dolly follows closely behind.

"*If you go down to the woods today,*
*You're sure of a big surprise.*
*If you go down to the woods today,*
*You'd better go in disguise.*"

As Dolly peeks from behind a tree,
She sees her friend with the Teddy Bear King.

With leapfrogging teddies under the trees,
The teddy bears play as they laugh and sing,

"For every bear that ever there was,
Is gathered there for certain,

Because today's the day
the teddy bears have their picnic."

The stars shine down on the party fun,
All the teddy bears are in fancy dress.
Ballerinas and wizards and cowboys,
A prince and a teddy bear princess.

As trees are draped with flags and balloons,

Teddy suddenly shouts out with glee,

"I can see you, Dolly, no need to hide!

Why not come to the party with me?"

At last, the midnight picnic begins,
There are marshmallows, jellies and cakes.

Dolly is the special guest of honour,
What a wonderful sight it all makes!

The guests have eaten all that they can,
Still, there's one final thing to be done.

The teddy bears dance to their very own song,
Dolly laughs and joins in with the fun.

As the teddy bears' picnic
draws to a close,
They know all good things
must come to an end.

Dolly says goodbye to the teddy bears,
Now it's time to go home with her friend.

Back home at last in their cosy beds,

The little friends yawn and snuggle up tight.

As they close their eyes and drift off to sleep,

They will dream of their magical night.